# That Girl In Black

## Mrs. Molesworth

Copyright © 2023 Culturea Editions
Text and cover : © public domain
Edition : Culturea (Hérault, 34)
Contact : infos@culturea.fr
Print in Germany by Books on Demand
Design and layout : Derek Murphy
Layout : Reedsy (https://reedsy.com/)
ISBN : 9791041826957
Légal deposit : July 2023

# That Girl In Black

## Chapter One.

He was spoilt—deplorably, absurdly spoilt. But, so far, that was perhaps the worst that could fairly be said against him. There was genuine manliness still, some chivalry even, yet struggling spasmodically to make itself felt, and—what was practically, perhaps, of more account as a preservative—some small amount of originality in his character. He had still a good deal to learn, and something too to unlearn before he could take rank as past-master in the stupid worldliness of his class and time. For he was neither so blasé nor so cynical as he flattered himself, but young enough to affect being both to the extent of believing his own affectations real.

He was popular; his position and income were fair enough to have secured this to a considerable extent in these, socially speaking, easy-going days, even had he been without the further advantages of good looks and a certain arrogance, not to say insolence of bearing, which, though nothing can be acquired with greater facility and at less expenditure of brain tissue, appears to be the one not-to-be-disputed hall-mark of the period.

Why he went to Mrs Englewood's reception that evening he could scarcely have told, or perhaps he would have vaguely shrunk from owning even to himself the real motives—of sincere though feeble loyalty to old associations, of faintly stirring gratitude for much kindness in the past—which had prompted the effort. For Mrs Englewood was neither very rich, nor very beautiful, nor—worst of "nors"—very fashionable; scarcely, indeed, to be reckoned as of notre monde in any very exclusive sense of the words, though kindly, and fairly refined, irreproachable as wife and mother, and so satisfied with her lot as to be uninterestingly free from social ambition.

But her house was commonplace, she herself not specially amusing.

"If she'd be content to ask me there when they're alone—I like talking to her herself well enough," thought Despard, as he dressed. In his heart, however, he knew that would not do. He was more or less of a lion from

Mrs Englewood's point of view; she was not above a certain pride in knowing that for "old sake's sake" she could count upon him for her one party of the season. And for this, as she retained a real affection for the man she had known as that delightful thing—a bright, intelligent, and unspoilt boy, and as she thought of him still far more highly than he deserved to be thought of, her conscience left her unrebuked.

Year after year, it is true, her husband wet-blanketed her innocent pleasure in seeing the young man's name on her invitation list.

"That fellow! In your place, my dear Gertrude!" and an expressive raising of the eyebrows said the rest.

"But, Harry," she would mildly expostulate, "you forget. I knew him when he was—"

"So high—at Whipmore. Oh, yes; I know all about it. Well, well, take your way of it; it doesn't hurt me if you invite people who don't want to come."

"But who always do come, you must allow," she would reply triumphantly.

"And think themselves mighty condescending for doing so," Mr Englewood put in.

"You don't do Despard justice. It's always the way with men, I suppose."

"Come now, don't be down upon me about it," he would say good-naturedly. "I don't stop your asking him. It isn't as if we had daughters. In that case—" but the rest was left to the imagination.

And this particular year Mrs Englewood had smiled to herself at this point of the discussion.

"One can make plans even though one hasn't daughters," she reflected. "If Harry would let me ask him to dinner now—but I know there's no chance of that. And, after all, a good deal may be done at an evening party. I should like to do Despard a good turn, and give him a start before any other. If I could give him a hint! But then there's my promise to her father,—and Despard is sure to be sensitive on those points. I might spoil it all. No; I shall appeal to his kindheartedness; that is the best. How tender he used to be to poor Lily when she was a tiny child! How he used to mount her up on his shoulders when she couldn't see the fireworks! I will tell Maisie that story! It is the sort of thing she will appreciate."

It was a hot, close evening. Though only May, there was thunder in the air, people said. Despard's inward dissatisfaction increased.

"Upon my soul it's too bad," he ejaculated while examining the flowers in his button-hole. "Why, when one's made up one's mind to do a disagreeable thing, should everything conspire to make it more odious than it need be, I wonder? I have really — more than half a mind — not to —"

Poor Gertrude Englewood, at that moment smilingly receiving her guests! She little knew how her great interest in the evening was trembling in the balance!

It was late when he arrived. Not that he had specially intended this. He cared too little about it to have considered whether he should be late or early, and, as he slowly made his way through the crowd at the doorway, he was conscious of but one wish — to get himself at once seen by his hostess, and then to make his escape as soon as possible. As to the first part of this little programme there was no difficulty. Scarcely did the first syllables of his name, "Mr Despard Norreys," fall on the ear, before Mrs Englewood's outstretched hand was in his, her pleasant face smiling up at him, her pleasant voice bidding him welcome. Yes, there was something difficult to resist about her; it was refreshing, somehow, and — there lay the secret — it brought back other days, when poor Jack's big sister, Gertrude, had welcomed the orphan schoolboy just as heartily, and when he had glowed with pride and gratification at her notice of him.

Despard's resigned, not to say sulky, expression cleared; it was no wonder Mrs Englewood's old liking for him had suffered no diminution; he did show at his best with her.

"So pleased you've come, so good of you," she was saying simply.

Her words made the young man feel vaguely ashamed of himself.

"Good of me!" he repeated, flushing a little, though the same or a much more fervent greeting from infinitely more exalted personages than

Gertrude had often failed to disturb his composure. "No, indeed, very much the reverse. I'm sorry," with a glance round, "to be so late, especially as—"

"No, no, you're not to begin saying you can't stay long, the very moment you've come. Listen, Despard," and she drew him aside a little; "I want you to do something to please me to-night. I have a little friend here—a Miss Fforde—that I want you to be very good to. Poor little thing, she's quite a stranger, knows nobody, never been out. But she's a nice little thing. Will you ask her to dance? or—" for the shadow of a frown on her favourite's forehead became evident even to Mrs Englewood's partial eyes—"if you don't care to dance, will you talk to her a little? Anything, you know, just to please her."

Despard bowed. What else could he do? Gertrude slid her hand through his arm.

"There she is," she said. "That girl in black over there by the fireplace. Maisie, my dear," for a step or two had brought them to the indicated spot, "I want to introduce my old friend, Mr Despard Norreys, to you. Mr Norreys—Miss Fforde;" and as she pronounced the names she drew her hand quietly away, and turned back towards her post at the door.

Despard bowed and, with the very slightest possible instinct of curiosity, glanced at the girl before him. She was of middle height, rather indeed under than above it; she was neither very fair nor very dark; there was nothing very special or striking in her appearance. She was dressed in black; there was nothing remarkable about her attire, rather, as Despard saw in an instant, an absence of style, of finish, which found its epithet at once in his thoughts—"countrified, of course," he said to himself. But before he had time to decide on his next movement she raised her eyes, and for half an instant his attention deepened. The eyes were strikingly fine; they were very blue, but redeemed from the shallowness of very blue eyes by the depth of the eyelashes, both upper and lower. And just now there was a brightness, an expectancy in the eyes which was by no means their constant expression. For, lashes notwithstanding, Miss Fforde's blue eyes could look cold enough when she chose.

"Good eyes," thought Despard. But just as he allowed the words to shape themselves in his brain, he noticed that over the girl's clear, pale face a glow of colour was quickly spreading.

"Good gracious!" he ejaculated mentally, "she is blushing! What a bread-and-butter miss she must be — to blush because a man's introduced to her. And I am to draw her out! It is really too bad of Mrs Englewood;" and he half began to turn away with a sensation of indignation and almost of disgust.

But positive rudeness where a woman was concerned did not come easy to him. He stopped, and muttered something indistinctly enough about "the pleasure of a dance." The girl had grown pale again by this time, and in her eyes a half startled, almost pained expression was replacing the glad expectancy. As he spoke, however, something of the former look returned to them.

"I — I shall be very pleased," she said. "I am not engaged for anything."

"I should think not," he said to himself. "I am quite sure you dance atrociously."

But aloud he said with the slow, impassive tone in which some of his admirers considered him so to excel that "Despard's drawl" had its school of followers —

"Shall we say the — the tenth waltz? I fear it is the first I can propose."

"Thank you," Miss Fforde replied. She looked as if she would have been ready to say more had he in the least encouraged it, but he, feeling that he had done his duty, turned away — the more eagerly as at that moment he caught sight in the crowd of a lady he knew.

"Mrs Marrinder! What a godsend!" he exclaimed.

He did not see Miss Fforde's face as he left her, and, had he done so, it would have taken far more than his very average modicum of discernment to have rightly interpreted the varying and curiously intermingling expressions which rapidly crossed it, like cloud shadows alternating with dashes of sunshine on an April morning. She stood for a moment or two where she was, then glancing round and seeing a vacant seat in a corner she quietly appropriated it.

"The tenth waltz," she repeated to herself with the ghost of a smile. "I wonder—" but that was all.

The evening wore on. Miss Fforde had danced once—but only once. It was with a man whom her host himself introduced to her, and, though good-natured and unaffected, he was boyish and commonplace; and she had to put some force on herself to reply with any show of interest to his attempts at conversation. She was engaged for one or two other dances, but it was hot, and the rooms were crowded, and with a scarcely acknowledged reflection—for Miss Fforde was young and inexperienced enough to think it hardly fair to make an engagement even for but a dance, to break it deliberately—that if her partners didnot find her it would not much matter, the girl withdrew quietly into a corner, where a friendly curtain all but screened her from observation, and allowed her to enjoy in peace the dangerous but delightful refreshment of an open window hard by.

The draught betrayed its source, however. She was scarcely seated when voices approaching caught her ears.

"Here you are—there must be a window open, it is ever so much cooler in this corner. Are you afraid of the draught?" said a voice she thought she recognised.

"No-o—at least—oh, this corner will do beautifully. The curtain will protect me. What a blessing to get a little air!" replied a second speaker—a lady evidently.

"People have no business to cram their rooms so. And these rooms are—well, not spacious. How in the world did you get Marrinder to come?"

The second speaker laughed. "It was quite the other way," she replied. "How did he get me to come? you might ask. He has something or other to do with our host, and made a personal matter of my coming, so, of course, I gave in."

"How angelic!"

"It is a penance; but we're going immediately."

"I shall disappear with you."

"You! Why you told me a moment ago that you were obliged to dance with some protégée of Mrs Englewood's — that she had made a point of it. And you haven't danced with her yet, to my certain knowledge," said the woman's voice again.

A sort of groan was the reply.

"Why, what's the matter?" with a light laugh.

"I had forgotten; you might have let me forget and go off with a clear conscience."

"What is there so dreadful about it?"

"It is that girl in black I have to dance with for my sins. Such a little dowdy. I am convinced she can't waltz. It was truly putting old friendship to the test to expect it of me. And of all things I do detest a bread-and-butter miss. You can see at a glance that this one has never left a country village before. She — "

But his further confidences were interrupted by the arrival of Mr Marrinder in search of his wife.

"You don't care to stay any longer, I suppose?" said the new-comer.

"Oh, — no; I am quite ready. I was engaged for this dance — the tenth, isn't it? But I am tired, and it doesn't matter. My partner, whoever he was, can find some one else. Good-night, Mr Norreys."

"Let me go with you to the door at least," he replied. "I'll look about for that girl in black on my way, so that if I don't see her I can honestly feel I have done my duty."

Then there came a flutter and rustling, and Miss Fforde knew that her neighbours had taken their departure.

She waited an instant, and then came out of her corner.

"He is not likely to come back to look for me in this room," she thought; "but in case he possibly should, I — I shall not hide myself."

She had had a moment's sharp conflict with herself before arriving at this decision; and her usually pale face was still faintly flushed when, slowly making his way in the direction of the sofa where she had now conspicuously placed herself, she descried Mr Norreys.

"Our dance — the tenth — I believe," he said, with an exaggeration of indifference, sounding almost as if he wished to irritate her into making some excuse to escape.

In her place nine girls out of ten would have done so, and without troubling themselves to hide their indignation. But Maisie Fforde was not one of those nine. She rose quietly from her seat and took his arm.

"Yes," she said, "it is our dance."

Something in her voice, or tone, made him glance at her with a shade more attention than he had hitherto condescended to bestow on "Mrs Englewood's protégée" She was looking straight before her; her features, which he now discovered to be delicate in outline, and almost faultlessly regular in their proportions, wore an expression of perfect composure; only the slight, very slight, rose-flush on her cheeks would have told to one who knew her well of some inward excitement.

"By Jove!" thought Despard, "she's almost pretty — no, pretty's not the word. I never saw a face quite like it before. I suppose I didn't look at her, she's so badly, at least so desperately plainly dressed. I don't, however, suppose she can talk, and I'd bet any money she can't dance."

As regarded the first of his predictions, she gave him at present no opportunity of judging. She neither spoke nor looked at him. He hazarded some commonplace remark about the heat of the rooms; she replied by a monosyllable. Despard began to get angry.

"Won't talk, whether she can or not," he said to himself, when a second observation had met with no better luck. He glanced round the room; all the other couples were either dancing, or smiling and talking. He became conscious of a curious sensation as disagreeable as novel — he felt as if he were looking ridiculous.

He turned again to his partner in a sort of desperation.

"Will you dance?" he said, and his tone was almost rough; it had entirely lost its usual calm, half-insolent indifference.

"Certainly," she said, while a scarcely perceptible smile faintly curved her lips. "It is, I suppose, what we are standing up here for, is it not?"

Despard grew furious. "She is laughing at me," he thought. "Impertinent little nobody. Where in Heaven's name has Gertrude Englewood unearthed her from? Upon my soul, it is the very last time she will see me at her dances!"

And somehow his discomfiture was not decreased by a glance, and almost involuntary glance, at Miss Fforde as they began to dance. She was certainly not striking in appearance; she was middle-sized, barely that indeed; her dress was now, he began to perceive, plain with the plainness of intention, not of ignorance or economy. But yet, with it all — no, he could not honestly feel that he was right; she did not look like "a nobody."

There was a further discovery in store for him. The girl danced beautifully. Mr Norreys imagined himself to have outlived all enthusiasm on such subjects, but now and then, in spite of the rôle which was becoming second nature to him, a bit of the old Despard — the hearty, unspoilt boy — cropped out, so to speak, unawares. This happened just now — his surprise had to do with it.

"You dance perfectly — exquisitely!" he burst out when at last they stopped. It was his second dance that evening only; neither he nor Miss Fforde was the least tired, and the room was no longer so crowded.

She looked up. There was no flush of gratification on her face, only a very slight — the slightest possible — sparkle in the beautiful eyes.

"Yes," she said quietly; "I believe I can dance well."

Despard bit his lips. For once in his life he felt absolutely at a loss what to say. Yet remain silent he would not, for by so doing it seemed to him as if he would be playing into the girl's hands.

"I will make her talk," he vowed internally.

It was not often he cared to exert himself, but he could talk, both intelligently and agreeably, when he chose to take the trouble. And gradually, though very gradually only, Miss Fforde began to thaw. She, too, could talk; though her words were never many, they struck him as remarkably well chosen and to the point. Yet more, they incited him to further effort. There was the restraint of power about them; not her words only, but her tone and expression, quick play of her features, the half-veiled glances of her eyes, were full of a curious fascination, seeming to tell how charming, how responsive a companion she might be if she chose.

But the fascination reacted as an irritant on Mr Norreys. He could not get rid of a mortifying sensation that he was being sounded, and his measure taken by this presumptuous little girl. Yet he glanced at her. No; "presumptuous" was not the word to apply to her. He grew almost angry at last, to the extent of nearly losing his self-control.

"You are drawing me out, Miss Ford," he said, "in hopes of my displaying my ignorance. You know much more about the book in question, and the subject, than I do. If you will be so good as to tell me all about it, I—"

She glanced up quickly with, for the first time, a perfectly natural and unconstrained expression on her face.

"Indeed—indeed, no," she said. "I am very ignorant. In some ways I have had little opportunity of learning."

Despard's face cleared. There was no question of her sincerity.

"I thought you were playing me off," he said boyishly.

Miss Fforde burst out laughing, but she instantly checked herself.

"What a pity," thought Mr Norreys. "I never heard a prettier laugh." "I did, indeed," he repeated, exaggerating his tone in hopes of making her laugh again.

But it was no use. Her face had regained the calm, formal composure it had worn at the beginning of the dance.

"She is like three girls rolled into one," thought Despard. "The shy, country-bred miss she seemed at first," and a feeling of shame shot through him at the recollection of his stupid judgment, "then this cold, impassive, princess-like damsel, and by fitful glimpses yet another, with nothing in common with either. And, notwithstanding the rôle she has chosen to play, I—I strongly suspect it is but a rôle," he decided hastily.

The riddle interested him.

"May I—will you not give me another dance?" he said deferentially. For the tenth waltz had come to an end.

"I am sorry I cannot," she replied. The words were simple and girlish, but the tone was regal. "Good-night, Mr Norreys. I congratulate you on your self-sacrifice at the altar of friendship. You may now take your departure with a clear conscience."

He stared. She was repeating some of his own words. Miss Fforde bowed coldly, and turned away. And Despard, bewildered, mortified even, though he would not own it, yet strangely attracted, and disgusted with himself for being so, after a passing word or two with his hostess, left the house.

An hour or two later Gertrude Englewood was bidding her young guest good-night.

"And oh, Maisie!" she exclaimed, "how did you get on with Despard? Is he not delightful?"

Miss Fforde smiled quietly. They were standing in her room, for she was to spend a night or two with her friend.

"I—to tell you the truth, I would much rather not speak about him," she said. "He is very good looking, and—well, not stupid, I dare say. But I am not used to men, you know, Gertrude—not to men of the day, at least, of which I suppose he is a type. I cannot say that I care to see more of them. I am happier at home with papa."

She turned away quickly. Gertrude did not see the tears that rose to the girl's eyes, or the rush of colour that overspread her face at certain recollections of that evening. She was nineteen, but it was her first "real" dance, and she felt as if years had passed since the afternoon only two days ago when she had arrived.

Mrs Englewood looked and felt sadly disappointed. She had been so pleased with her own diplomacy.

"It will be different when you are a little more in the way of it," she said. "And—I really don't think your father should insist on your dressing quite so plainly. It will do the very thing he wants to avoid—it will make you remarkable."

"No, no," said Maisie, shaking her head. "Papa is quite right. You must allow it had not that effect this evening. No one asked to be introduced to me."

"There was such a crowd—" Gertrude began, but this time Maisie's smile was quite a hearty one as she interrupted her.

"Never mind about that," she said. "But do tell me one thing. I saw Mr Norreys speaking to you for a moment as he went out. You didn't say anything about me to him, I hope?"

"No," said Mrs Englewood, "I did not. I would have liked to do so," she added honestly, "but somehow he looked queer—not exactly bored, but not encouraging. So I just let him go."

"That's right," said Maisie; "thank you. I am so glad you didn't. I do hope I shall never see him again," she added to herself.

**Chapter Two.**

A hope not destined to be fulfilled.

For though Maisie wrote home to "papa" the morning after Mrs Englewood's dance, earnestly begging for leave to return to the country at once instead of going on to her next visit, and assuring him that she felt she would never be happy in fashionable society, never be happy anywhere, indeed, away from him and everything she cared for, papa was inexorable. It was natural she should be homesick at first, he replied; natural, and indeed unavoidable, that she should feel strange and lonely; and, as she well knew, she could not possibly long more, to be with him again, than he longed to have her; but there were all the reasons she knew full well why she should stay in town as had been arranged; the very reasons which had made him send her now made him say she must remain. Her own good sense would show her the soundness of his motives, and she must behave like his own brave Maisie. And the girl never knew what this letter had cost her invalid father, nor how he shrank from opposing her wishes.

"She set off so cheerfully," he said to himself, "and she has only been there three days. And she seemed rather to have enjoyed her first dinner-party and the concert, or whatever it was, that Gertrude Englewood took her to. What can have happened at the evening party? She dances well, I know; and she is not the sort of girl to expect or care much about ball-room admiration."

Poor man! it was, so far, a disappointment to him. He would have liked to get a merry, happy letter that morning as he sat at his solitary breakfast. For he had no fear, no shadow of a fear, that his Maisie's head ever could be turned.

"I have guarded against any dangers of that kind for her, at least," he said to himself, "provided I have not gone too far and made her too sober-minded. But no; after all, it is erring on the safe side — considering everything."

Three or four evenings after Mrs Englewood's dance Despard found himself at a musical party. He was in his own milieu this time, and proportionately affable—with the cool, condescending affability which was the nearest approach to making himself agreeable that he recognised. He had been smiled at by the beauty of the evening, much enjoying her discomfiture when he did not remain many minutes by her side; he had been all but abjectly entreated by the most important of the dowagers, a very great lady indeed, in every sense of the word, to promise his assistance at her intended theatricals; he had, in short, received the appreciation which was due to him, and was now resting on his oars, comfortably installed in an easy chair, debating within himself whether it was worth while to give Mrs Belmont a fright by engrossing her pretty daughter, and thus causing to retire from her side in the sulks Sir Henry Gayburn, to whom the girl was talking. For Sir Henry was rich, and was known to be looking out for a wife, and Despard had long since been erased from the maternal list of desirable possibilities.

"Shall I?" he was saying to himself as he lay back with a smile, when a voice beside him made him look up. It was that of the son of the house, a friend of his own; the young man seemed annoyed and perplexed.

"Norreys! oh, do me a good turn, will you? I have to look after the lady who has just been singing, and my mother is fussing about a girl who has been sitting all the evening alone. She's a stranger. Will you be so awfully good as to take her down for an ice or something?"

Despard looked round. He could scarcely refuse a request so couched, but he was far from pleased.

"Where is she? Who is she?" he asked, beginning languidly to show signs of moving.

"There—over by the window—that girl in black," his friend replied. "Who she is I can't say. My mother told me her name was Ford. Come along, and I'll introduce you, that's a good fellow."

Despard by this time had risen to his feet.

"Upon my soul!" he ejaculated.

But Mr Leslie was in too great a hurry to notice the unusual emphasis with which he spoke.

And in half a second he found himself standing in front of the girl, who, the last time they met, had aroused in him such unwonted emotions.

"Miss Ford," murmured young Leslie, "may I introduce Mr Norreys?" and then Mr Leslie turned on his heel and disappeared.

Despard stood there perfectly grave. He would hazard no repulse; he waited for her.

She looked up, but there was no smile on her face—only the calm self-composedness which it seemed to him he knew so well. How was it so? Had he met her before in some former existence? Why did all about her seem at once strange and yet familiar? He had never experienced the like before.

These thoughts—scarcely thoughts indeed—flickered through his brain as he looked at her. They served one purpose at least, they prevented his feeling or looking awkward, could such a state of things have been conceived possible.

Seeing that he was not going to speak, remembering, perhaps, that if he remembered the last words she had honoured him with, he could scarcely be expected to do so, she at last opened her lips.

"That," she said quietly, slightly inclining her head in the direction where young Leslie had stood, "was, under the circumstances, unnecessary."

"He did not know," said Despard.

"I suppose not; though I don't know. Perhaps you told him you had forgotten my name."

"No," he replied, "I did not. It would not have been true."

She smiled very slightly.

"There is no dancing to-night," she said. "May I ask—?" and she hesitated.

"Why I ventured to disturb you?" he interrupted. "I was requested to take you downstairs for an ice or whatever you may prefer to that. The farce did not originate with me, I assure you."

"Do you mean by that that you will not take me downstairs?" she said, smiling again as she got up from her seat. "I should like an ice very much."

Despard bowed without speaking, and offered her his arm.

But when he had piloted her through the crowd, and she was standing quietly with her ice, he broke the silence.

"Miss Ford," he began, "as the fates have again forced me on your notice, I should like to ask you a question."

She raised her eyes inquiringly. No — he had not exaggerated their beauty.

"I should like to know the meaning of the strange words you honoured me with as I was leaving Mrs Englewood's the other evening. I do not think you have forgotten them."

"No," she replied, "I have not forgotten them, and I meant them, and I still mean them. But I will not talk about them or explain anything I said."

There was nothing the least flippant in her tone — only quiet determination. But Despard, watching keenly, saw that her lips quivered a little as she spoke.

"As you choose," he said. "Of course, in the face of such a very uncompromising refusal, I can say nothing more."

"Then shall we go upstairs again?" proposed Miss Fforde.

Mr Norreys acquiesced. But he had laid his plans, and he was a more diplomatic adversary than Miss Fforde was prepared to cope with.

"I finished reading the book we were speaking of the other evening," he began in a matter-of-fact voice; "I mean —" and he named the book. "At least, I fancy it was you I was discussing it with. The last volume falls off greatly."

"Oh, do you think so?" said the girl in a tone of half-indignant disappointment, falling blindly into the trap. "I, on the contrary, felt that the last volume made amends for all that was unsatisfactory in the others. You see by it what he was driving at all the time, and that the persiflage and apparent cynicism were only means to an end. I do hate cynicism — it is so easy, and such a little makes such a great effect."

Something in her tone made Despard feel irritated. "Is she hitting at me again?" he thought. And the idea threw him, in his turn, off his guard.

The natural result was that both forgot themselves in the interest of the discussion. And Despard, when he, as it were, awoke to the realisation of this, took care not to throw away the advantage he had gained. He drew her out, he talked as he but seldom exerted himself to do, and when, at the end of half-an-hour or so, an elderly lady, whom he knew by name only, was seen approaching them, and Miss Fforde sprang to her feet, exclaiming, —

"Have you been looking for me? I hope not —" he smiled quietly as he prepared to withdraw — he had succeeded!

"Good-night, Mr Norreys," said Maisie simply.

"Two evenings ago she would not say good-night at all," he thought. But he made no attempt to do more than bow quietly.

"You are very — cold, grim — no, I don't know what to call it, Maisie, dear," said the lady, her cousin and present chaperone, as they drove away, "in your manner to men; and that man in particular — Despard Norreys. It is not often he is so civil to any girl."

"I detest all men — all young men," replied Maisie irritably.

"But, my dear, you should be commonly civil. And he had been giving himself, for him, unusual trouble to entertain you."

"Can he know about her? Oh, no, it is impossible," she added to herself.

Miss Fforde closed her lips firmly. But in a moment or two she opened them again.

"Cousin Agnes," she said, half smiling, "I am afraid you are quite mistaken. If I had not been what you call 'commonly civil,' would he have gone on talking to me? On the contrary, I am sadly afraid I was far too civil."

"My dear child," ejaculated her cousin, "what do you mean?"

"Oh," said Maisie, "I don't know. Never mind the silly things I say. I like being with you, Cousin Agnes, but I don't like London. I am much happier at home in the country."

"But, my dear child, when I saw you at home a few months ago you were looking forward with pleasure to coming. What has changed you? What has disappointed you?"

"I am not suited for anything but a quiet country life—that is all," said Miss Fforde.

"But, then, Maisie, afterwards, you know, you will have to come to town and have a house of your own and all that sort of thing. It is necessary for you to see something of the world to prepare you for—"

"Afterwards isn't now, Cousin Agnes. And I am doing my best, as papa wished," said the girl weariedly. "Do let us talk of something else. Really sometimes I do wish I were any one but myself."

"Maisie," said her cousin reproachfully, "you know, dear, that isn't right. You must take the cares and responsibilities of a position like yours along with the advantages and privileges of it."

"I know," Miss Fforde replied meekly enough; "but, Cousin Agnes, do tell me who was that very funny-looking man with the long fluffy beard whom you were talking to for some time."

"Oh, that, my dear, was Count Dalmiati, the celebrated so-and-so," and once launched in her descriptions Cousin Agnes left Maisie in peace.

Two days later came the afternoon of Lady Valence's garden-party. It was one of the garden parties to which "everybody" went—Despard Norreys for one, as a matter of course. He had got more gratification and less annoyance out of his second meeting with Miss Fforde; for he flattered himself he knew how to manage her now—"that little girl in black, who thinks herself so wonderfully wise, forsooth!" Yet the sting was there still; the very persistence with which he repeated to himself that he had mastered her showed it. His thoughts recurred to her more than they were in the habit of doing to any one or anything but his own immediate concerns. Out of curiosity, merely, no doubt; curiosity increased by the apparent improbability of satisfying it. For no one seemed to know anything about her. She might have dropped from the skies. He had indeed some difficulty in recalling her personality to the two or three people to whom he applied for information.

"A girl in black—at the Leslies' musical party? Why, my dear fellow, there were probably a dozen girls in black there. There usually is a good sprinkling of black frocks at evening parties," said one of the knowers of everybody whom he had selected to honour with his inquiries. "What was there remarkable about her? There must have been something to attract your notice."

"No, on the contrary," Despard replied, "she was remarkably unremarkable;" and he laughed lightly. "It was only rather absurd. I have seemed haunted by her once or twice lately, and yet nobody knows anything about her, except that her name is Ford."

"Ford," said his companion; "that does not tell much. And not pretty, you say?"

"Pretty, oh, yes. No, not exactly pretty," and a vision of Maisie's clear cold profile and—yes, there was no denying it—mostlovely eyes, rose before him. "More than pretty," he would have said had he not been afraid of being laughed at. "I don't really know how to describe her, and it is of less than no consequence. I don't suppose I shall ever see her again," and he went on to talk of other matters.

He did see her again, however, and it was, as will have already been supposed, at Lady Valence's garden-party that he did so. It was a cold day, of course. The weather, with its usual consideration, had changed that very morning, after having been, for May, really decently mild and agreeable. The wind had veered round to the east, and it seemed not improbable that the rain would look in, an uninvited guest, in the course of the afternoon.

Lady Valence declared herself in despair, but as nobody could remember the weather ever being anything but highly detestable the day of her garden-party, it is to be hoped that she in reality took it more philosophically than she allowed, Despard strode about feeling very cold, and wondering why he had come, and why, having come, he stayed. There was a long row of conservatories and ferneries, and glass-houses of every degree of temperature not far from the lawn, where at one end the band was playing, and at the other some deluded beings were eating ices. Despard shivered; the whole was too ghastly. A door in the centre house stood invitingly open, and he turned in. Voices near at hand, female voices, warned him off at one side, for he was not feeling amiable, and he hastened in the opposite direction. By degrees the pleasant warmth, the extreme beauty of the plants and flowers amidst which he found himself, the solitariness, too, soothed and subdued his irritation.

"If I could smoke," he began to say to himself, when, looking round with a half-formed idea of so doing, he caught sight amidst the ferns of feminine drapery. Some one was there before him—but a very quiet, mouse-like somebody. A somebody who was standing there motionless, gazing at the tall tropical plants, enjoying, apparently, the warmth and the quiet like himself.

"That girl in black, that sphinx of a girl again—by Jove!" murmured Despard under his breath, and as he did so, she turned and saw him.

Her first glance was of annoyance; he saw her clearly from where he stood, there was no mistaking the fact. But, so quickly, that it was difficult to believe it had been there, the expression of vexation passed. The sharply contracted brows smoothed; the graceful head bent slightly forward; the lips parted.

"How do you do, Mr Norreys?" she said. "We are always running against each other unexpectedly, are we not?"

Her tone was perfectly natural, her manner expressed simple pleasure and gratification. She was again the third, the rarest of her three selves—the personality which Despard, in his heart of hearts, believed to be herself.

He smiled—a slightly amused, almost a slightly condescending smile, but a very pleasant one all the same. He could afford to be pleasant now. Poor silly little girl—she had given in with a good grace, a truce to her nonsense of regal airs and dignity; a truce, too, to the timid self-consciousness of her first introduction.

"She understands better now, I see," he thought. "Understands that a little country girl is but—ah, well—but a little country girl. Still, I must allow—" and he hesitated as his glance fell on her; it was the first time he had seen her by daylight, and the words he had mentally used did not quite "fit"— "I must allow that she has brains, and some character of her own."

"I can imagine its seeming so to you," he said aloud. "You have, I think you told me, lived always in the country. Of course, in the country one's acquaintances stand out distinctly, and one remembers every day whom one has and has not seen. In town it is quite different. I find myself constantly forgetting people, and doing all sorts of stupid things, imagining I have seen some one last week when it was six months ago, and so on. But people are really very good-natured."

She listened attentively.

"How difficult it must be to remember all the people you know!" she said, with the greatest apparent simplicity; indeed, with a tone of almost awe-struck reverence.

"I simply don't attempt it," he replied.

"How—dear me, I hardly know how to say it—how very good and kind of you it is to remember me," she said.

Mr Norreys glanced at her sharply.

Was she playing him off? For an instant the appalling suggestion all but took his breath away, but it was quickly dismissed. Its utter absurdity was too self-evident; and the expression on her face reassured him. She seemed so innocent as she stood there, her eyes hidden for the moment by their well-fringed lids, for she was looking down. A faint, the very faintest, suspicion of a blush coloured her cheeks, there was a tiny little trembling about the corners of her mouth. But somehow these small evidences of confusion did not irritate him as they had done when he first met her. On the contrary. "Poor little girl," he said to himself. "I see I must be careful. Still, she will live to get over it, and one cannot be positively brutal."

For an instant or two he did not speak.

Then: "I never pay compliments, Miss Ford," he said, "but what I am going to say may sound to you like one. However, I trust you will not dislike it."

And again he unaccountably hesitated — what was the matter with him? He meant to be kindly encouraging to the girl, but as she stood beside him, looking up with a half-curious, half-deprecating expression in her eyes, he was conscious of his face slightly flushing; the words he wanted refused to come, he felt as if he were bewitched.

"Won't you tell me what you were going to say?" she said at last. "I should so like to hear it."

"It's not worth saying," he blurted out. "Indeed, though I know what I mean, I cannot express it. You — you are quite different from other girls, Miss Ford. It would be impossible to confuse you with the crowd. That's about the sum of what I was thinking, though — I meant to express it differently. Certainly, in the way I have said it, no one by any possibility could take it for a compliment."

To his surprise she looked up at him with a bright smile, a smile of pleasure, and — of something else.

"On the contrary, I do take it as a compliment, as a very distinct compliment," she said, "considering whom it comes from. Though, after all, it is scarcely I that should accept it. The — the circumstances of my life may have made me different — my having been so little in town, for instance. I suppose there are some advantages in everything, even in apparent disadvantages."

Her extreme gentleness and deference put him at his ease again.

"Oh, certainly," he said. "For my part, I often wish I had never been anywhere or seen anything! Life would, in such a case, seem so much more interesting. There would be still things left to dream about."

He sighed, and there was something genuine in his sigh. "I envy people who have never travelled, sometimes," he added.

"Have you travelled much?" she asked.

"Oh, dear, yes — been everywhere — the usual round."

"But the usual round is just what with me counts for nothing," she said sharply. "Real travelling means living in other countries, leading the life of their peoples, not rushing round the capitals of Europe from one cosmopolitan hotel to another."

He smiled a superior smile. "When you have rushed round the capitals of Europe you may give an opinion," his smile seemed to say.

"That sort of thing is impossible, except for Bohemians," he said languidly. "I detest talking about travels."

"Do you really?" she said, with a very distinct accent of contempt. "Then I suppose you have not read —" and she named a book on everybody's table at the moment.

Despard's face lighted up.

"Oh, indeed, yes," he said. "That is not an ordinary book of travels;" and he went on to speak of the volume in question in a manner which showed that he had read it intelligently, while Miss Fforde, forgetting herself and her companion in the interest of what he said, responded sympathetically.

Half unconsciously, as they talked they strolled up and down the wide open space in front of the ferns. Suddenly voices, apparently approaching them, caught the girl's ear.

"Oh, dear," she said, "my friends will be wondering what has become of me! I must go. Good-bye, Mr Norreys," and she held out her hand. There was something simple and perfectly natural in her manner as she did so, which struck him. It was almost as if she were throwing off impulsively a part which she was tired of playing.

He held her hand for a quarter of an instant longer than was actually necessary.

"I—I hope we may meet again, Miss Ford," he said, simply but cordially—something in her present manner was infectious—"and continue our talk."

She glanced up at him.

"I hope so, too," she said quickly. But then her brows contracted again a little. "At least—I don't know that it is very probable," she added disconnectedly, as she hastened away in the direction whence came the voices.

"Hasn't many invitations, I dare say," he said to himself as he looked after her. "If she had been still with Gertrude Englewood I might, perhaps, have got one or two people to be civil to them. But I daresay it would have been Quixotic, and it's the sort of thing I dislike doing—putting one's self under obligation for no real reason."

If he had heard what Maisie Fforde was thinking to herself as she made her way quickly to her cousin!

"What a pity!" she thought. "What a real pity that a man who must have had good material in him should have so sunk—to what I can't help thinking vulgarity of feeling, if not of externals—to such contemptible self-conceit and affectations! I can understand, however, that he may have been a nice boy once, as Gertrude maintains. Poor Gertrude—how her hero has turned out! I must never let her know how impossible I find it to resist drawing him out—it surely is not wrong? Oh, how I should love to see him thoroughly humbled! The worst of it is, that when he becomes a reasonable being, as he does now and then, he can be so nice—interesting even—and I forget whom I am talking to. But not for long! No, indeed—'Mrs Englewood's dowdy protégée,' the 'bread-and-butter miss,' for whom the tenth waltz was too much condescension, hasn't such a bad memory. And when I had looked forward to my first dance so, and fancied the world was a good and kind place! Oh!" and she clenched her hands as the hot mortification, the scathing désillusionnement, of that evening recurred to her in its full force. "Oh, I hope it is not wicked and un-Christian, but I should love to see him humbled! I wonder if I shall meet him again. I hope not—and yet I hope I shall."

The "again" came next at a dinner-party, to which she accompanied her cousin. Mrs Maberly was old-fashioned in some of her ideas. Nothing, for instance, would persuade her that it was courteous to be more than twenty minutes later than the dinner-hour named, in consequence of which she not unfrequently found herself the first arrival. This in no way annoyed Maisie, as it might have done a less simple-minded maiden; indeed, on the contrary, it rather added to her enjoyment. She liked to get into a quiet corner and watch the various guests as they came in; she felt amused by, and yet sorry for, the little perturbations she sometimes discerned on the part of the hostess, especially if the latter happened to be young and at all anxious-minded. This was the case on the evening in question, when fully half-an-hour had been spent by Miss Fforde in her corner before dinner was announced.

"It is too bad," Maisie overhead the young châtelaine whisper to a friend, "such affectation really amounts to rudeness. But yet it is so awkward to go down—" then followed some words too low for her to understand, succeeded by a joyful exclamation—"Ah, there he is at last," as again the door opened, and "Mr Norreys" was announced.

And Maisie's ears must surely have been praeter-naturally sharp, for through the buzz of voices, through the hostess's amiably expressed reproaches, they caught the sound of her own name, and the fatal words "that girl in black."

"You must think me a sort of Frankenstein's nightmare," she could not help saying with a smile, as Despard approached to take her down to dinner. But she was scarcely prepared for the rejoinder.

"I won't contradict you, Miss Ford, if you like to call yourself names. No, I should have been both surprised and disappointed had you not been here. I have felt sure all day I was going to meet you."

Maisie felt herself blush, felt too that his eyes were upon her, and blushed more, in fury at herself.

"Fool that I am," she thought. "He is going to play now at making me fall in love with him, is he? How contemptible, how absurd! Does he really imagine he can take me in?"

She raised her head proudly and looked at him, to show him that she was not afraid to do so. But the expression on his face surprised her again. It was serious, gentle, and almost deprecating, yet with an honest light in the eyes such as she had never seen there before.

"What an actor he would make," she thought. But a little quiver of some curious inexplicable sympathy which shot through her as she caught those eyes, belied the unspoken words.

"I am giving far more thought to the man and his moods than he is worth," was the decision she had arrived at by the time they reached the dining-room door. "After all, the wisest philosophy is to take the goods the gods send us and enjoy them. I shall forget it all for the present, and speak to him as to any other pleasant man I happen to meet."

And for that evening, and whenever they met, which was not unfrequently in the course of the next few weeks, Maisie Fforde kept to this determination. It was not difficult, for when he chose, Despard Norreys could be more than pleasant. And—"Miss Ford" in her third personality was not hard to be pleasant to; and—another "and"—they were both young, both—in certain directions—deplorably mistaken in their estimates of themselves; and, lastly, human nature is human nature still, through all the changes of philosophies, fashions, and customs.

The girl was no longer acting a part; had she been doing so, indeed, she could not so perfectly have carried out the end she had, in the first fire of her indignation, vaguely proposed to herself. For the time being she was, so to speak, "letting herself go" with the pleasant insidious current of circumstances.

Yet the memory of that first evening was still there. She had not forgotten.

And Despard?

## Chapter Three.

The London season was over. Mr Norreys had been longing for its close; so, at least, he had repeated to his friends, and with even more insistence to himself, a great many, indeed a very great many, times, during the last hot, dusty weeks of the poor season's existence. He wanted to get off to Norway in a friend's yacht for some fishing, he said; he seemed for once really eager about it, so eager as to make more than one of his companions smile, and ask themselves what had come to Norreys, he who always took things with such imperturbable equanimity, what had given him this mania for northern fishing?

And now the fishing and the trip were things of the past. They had not turned out as delightful in reality as in anticipation somehow, and yet what had gone wrong Despard, on looking back, found it hard to say. That nothing had gone wrong was the truth of the matter. The weather had been fine and favourable; the party had been well chosen; Lennox-Brown, the yacht's owner, was the perfection of a host.

"It was a case of the workman, not of the tools, I suspect," Despard said to himself one morning, when, strolling slowly up and down the smooth bit of gravel path outside the drawing-room windows at Markerslea Vicarage, he allowed his thoughts to wander backwards some little way. "I am sick of it all," he went on, with an impatient shake, testifying to inward discomposure. "I'm a fool after all, no wiser, indeed a very great deal more foolish, than my neighbours. And I've been hard enough upon other fellows in my time. Little I knew! I cannot throw it off, and what to do I know not."

He was staying with his sister, his only near relation. She was older than he, had been married for several years, and had but one trouble in life. She was childless. Naturally, therefore, she lavished on Despard an altogether undue amount of sisterly devotion. But she was by no means an entirely foolish woman. She had helped to spoil him, and she was beginning to regret it.

"He is terribly, quite terribly blasé," she was saying to herself as she watched him this morning, herself unobserved. "I have never seen it so plainly as this autumn," and she sighed. "He is changed, too; he is moody and irritable, and that is new. He has always been so sweet-tempered. Surely he has not got into money difficulties—I can scarcely think so. He is too sensible. Though, after all, as Charles often says, perhaps the best thing that could befall the poor boy would be to have to work hard for his living—" a most natural remark on the part of "Charles," seeing that he himself had always enjoyed a thoroughly comfortable sufficiency,—and again Mrs Selby sighed.

Her sigh was echoed; she started slightly, then, glancing round, she saw that the glass door by which she stood was ajar, and that her brother had arrested his steps for a moment or two, and was within a couple of yards of her. It was his sigh that she had heard. Her face clouded over still more; it is even probable that a tear or two rose unbidden to her eyes. She was a calm, considering woman as a rule; for once she yielded to impulse, and, stepping out, quickly slipped her hand through Mr Norreys' arm.

"My dear Despard," she said, "what a sigh! It sounded as if from the very depths of your heart, if," she went on, trying to speak lightly, "if you have one that is to say, which I have sometimes doubted."

But he threw back no joke in return.

"I have never given you reason to doubt it, surely, Maddie?" he said half reproachfully.

"No, no, dear. I'm in fun, of course. But seriously—"

"I'm serious enough."

"Yes, that you are—too serious. What's the matter, Despard, for that there is something the matter I am convinced?"

He did not attempt to deny it.

"Yes, Madeline," he said slowly, "I'm altogether upset. I've been false to all my own theories. I've been a selfish enough brute always, I know, but at least I think I've been consistent. I've chosen my own line, and lived the life, and among the people that suited me, and—"

"Been dreadfully, miserably spoilt, Despard."

He glanced up at her sharply. No, she was not smiling. His face clouded over still more.

"And that's the best even you can say of me?" he asked.

Mrs Selby hardly let him finish.

"No, no. I am blaming myself more than you," she said quickly. "You are much—much better than you know, Despard. You are not selfish really. Think of what you have done for others; how consistently you have given up those evenings to that night school."

"One a week—what's that? And there's no credit in doing a thing one likes. I enjoy those evenings, and it's more than I can say for the average of my days."

But his face cleared a very little as he spoke.

"Well," she went on, "that shows you are not at heart an altogether selfish brute," and now she smiled a little. "And all the more does it show how much better you might still be if you chose. I am very glad, delighted, Despard, that you arediscontented and dissatisfied; I knew it would come sooner or later."

Mr Norreys looked rather embarrassed.

"Maddie," he began again, "you haven't quite understood me. I didn't finish my sentence. I was going on to say that at least I had done no harm to anyone else; if no one's any better through me, at least no one's the worse for my selfishness—oh, yes, don't interrupt," he went on. "I know what you'd like to say—'No man liveth to himself,' the high-flown sort of thing. I don't go in for that. But now—I have not even kept my consistency. You'd never guess what I've gone and done—at least, Maddie, canyou guess?"

And his at all times sweet voice sweetened and softened as he spoke, and into his eyes stole a look Madeline had never seen there before.

"Despard," she exclaimed breathlessly, "have you, can you, have you fallen in love?"

He nodded.

"Oh, dear Despard," she exclaimed, "I am so very glad. It will be the making of you. That's to say, if—but it must be somebodyvery nice."

"Nice enough in herself—nice," he repeated, and he smiled. "Yes, if by nice you mean everything sweet and womanly, and original and delightful, and—oh, you mustn't tempt me to talk about her. But what she is herself is not the only thing, my poor Maddie."

Mrs Selby gave a start.

"Oh, Despard," she exclaimed, "you don't mean that she's a married woman."

"No, no."

"Or, or any one very decidedly beneath you?" she continued, with some relief, but anxiously still.

Despard hesitated.

"That's exactly what I can't quite say," he replied. "She's a lady by birth, that I'm sure of. But she has seen very little. Lived always in a village apparently—she has been in some ways unusually well and carefully educated. But I'm quite positive she's poor, really with nothing of her own, I fancy. I'm not sure—it has struck me once or twice that perhaps she had been intended for a governess."

Mrs Selby gasped, but checked herself.

"She has friends who are kind to her. I met her at some good houses. It was at Mrs Englewood's first of all, but since then I've seen her at much better places."

"But why do you speak so doubtfully—you keep saying 'I fancy'—'I suppose.' It must be easy to find out all about her."

"No; that's just it. She's curiously, no—not reserved—she's too nice and well-bred for that sort of thing—but, if you can understand, she's frankly backward in speaking of herself. She'll talk of anything but herself. She has an old invalid father whom she adores—and—upon my soul, that's about all she has ever told me."

"You can ask Mrs Englewood, surely."

Despard frowned.

"I can, and I have; at least, I tried it. But it was not easy. She's been rather queer to me lately. She would volunteer no information, and of course—you see—I didn't want to seem interested on the subject. It's only just lately, since I came here in fact, that I've really owned it to myself," and his face flushed. "I went yachting and fishing to put it out of my head, but—it's been no use—I won't laugh at all that sort of thing again as I have done, I can tell you."

"He's very much in earnest," thought Mrs Selby.

"What—you don't mind telling me—what is her name?" she asked.

"Ford—Miss Ford. I fancy her first name is Mary. There's a pet name they call her by," but he did not tell it.

"Mary Ford—that does not sound aristocratic," mused Mrs Selby. "Despard, tell me—Mrs Englewood is really fond of you. Do you think she knows anything against the girl, or her family, or anything like that, and that she was afraid of it for you?"

"Oh, dear no! Quite the contrary, Mai—Miss Ford is a great pet of hers. Gertrude was angry with me for not being civil to her," and he laughed.

"Not being civil to her," she repeated. "And you were falling in love with her? How do you mean?"

"That was afterwards. I was brutally uncivil to her at first. That's how it began somehow," he said, disconnectedly.

Mrs Selby felt utterly perplexed. Was he being taken in by a designing girl? It all sounded very inconsistent.

"Despard," she said after a little silence, "shall I try to find out all about her from Mrs Englewood? She would not refuse any information if it was for your sake."

He considered.

"Well, yes," he said, "perhaps you'd better."

"And—" she went on, "if all is satisfactory—"

"Well?"

"You will go through with it?"

"I—suppose so. Altogether satisfactory it can't be. I'm fairly well off as a bachelor, but that's a very different matter. And—Maddie—I should hate poverty."

"You would have no need to call it poverty," she said rather coldly.

"Well—well—I'm speaking comparatively of course," he replied, impatiently. "It would be what I call poverty. And I am selfish, I know. The best of me won't come out under those circumstances. I've no right to marry, you see—that's what's been tormenting me."

"But if she likes to face it—would not that bring out the best of you?" said Mrs Selby hopefully, though in her heart rather shocked by his way of speaking.

"Perhaps—I can't say. But of course if she did—"

"And you are sure she would?" asked Madeline, suddenly awaking to the fact that Miss Ford's feelings in the matter had been entirely left out of the question.

Despard smiled.

"Do you mean am I sure she cares for me?" he said. "Oh, yes—as for that—"

"I don't like a girl who—who lets it be seen if she cares for a man," she said.

Mr Norreys turned upon her.

"Lets it be seen," he repeated angrily. "Maddie, you put things very disagreeably. Would I—tell me, is it likely that I would take to a girl so utterly devoid of delicacy as your words sound? And is it so improbable that a girl would care for me?" He smiled in spite of himself, and Mrs Selby's answering smile as she murmured: "I did not mean that, you know," helped to smooth him down. "She did her best to make me think she detested me," he added. "But—"

"Ah, yes, but—" said his sister fondly. "Then it is settled, Despard," she went on. "I shall tackle Mrs Englewood in my own way. You can trust me. You don't know where Miss Ford is at present?" she added.

He shook his head despondently.

"Not the ghost of an idea. I didn't try to hear. I thought I didn't want to know, you see. But—Maddie," he added, half timidly, "you'll write at once?"

"As soon as I possibly can," she replied kindly, for glancing at him she saw that he looked really ill and worn. "And," she went on, "as my reward, you will go with me to the Densters' garden-party this afternoon. Charles can't, and I hate going alone. I don't know them—it is their first year here, though everybody says they are very nice people."

"Oh, dear," said Despard. "Very well, Maddie. I must, I suppose."

"Then be ready at a quarter to four. I'll drive you in the pony-carriage," and Madeline disappeared through the glass door whence she had emerged.

"I wonder if she will write to-day," thought Mr Norreys, though he would have been ashamed to ask it. "I should like to know it's done—a sort of crossing the Rubicon. And it's a good while now since that last day I saw her. She was never quite so sweet as that day. Supposing I heard she was married?"

His heart seemed to stop beating at the thought, and he grew white, though there was no one to see. But he reassured himself. Few things were less likely. Portionless girls, however charming, don't marry so quickly nowadays.

Madeline's feelings were mingled. She was honestly and unselfishly glad of what she believed might be a real turning point towards good for Despard. Yet—"if only he had not chosen a girl quite so denuded of worldly advantages as she evidently is," she reflected. "For of course if she had either money or connection Mrs Englewood would not have kept it a secret. She is far too outspoken. I must beg her to tell everything she knows, not to be afraid of my mixing her name up in the matter in any way. When she sees that Charles and I do not disapprove she will feel less responsibility."

And it was with a comfortable sense of her own and "Charles's" unworldliness that Mrs Selby prepared to indite the important letter.

She saw little of her brother till the afternoon. He did not appear at luncheon, having left word that he had gone for a long walk.

"Provided only that he is not too late for the Densters'," thought Madeline, with a little sigh over the perversity of mankind.

But her fears were unfounded. At ten minutes to four Mr Norreys made his appearance in the hall, faultlessly attired, apologising with his usual courtesy, in which to his sister he never failed, for his five minutes' delay, and Mrs Selby, feeling pleased with herself outwardly and inwardly, for she was conscious both of looking well in a very pretty new bonnet, and of acting a truly high-minded part as a sister, seated herself in her place, with a glance of satisfaction at her companion.

"Everybody will be envying me," she said to herself, with a tiny sigh as she remembered former air-castles in Despard's behoof. "The Flores-Carter girls and Edith and Bertha Byder, indeed all the neighbourhood get quite excited if they know he's here. He might have had his choice of the best matches in this county, to my own knowledge, and there are several girls with money. Ah, well!"

The grounds seemed already fall of guests when the brother and sister drove up to the Densters' door. Mrs Selby was at once seized upon by some of her special cronies, and for half an hour or so Despard kept dutifully beside her, allowing himself to be introduced to any extent, doing his best to please his sister by responding graciously to the various attentions which were showered upon him. But he grew very tired of it all in a little while — a curious dreamy feeling began to come over him, born no doubt of the unwonted excitement of his conversation with Madeline that morning.

He had gone a long walk in hopes of recovering his usual equanimity, but had only succeeded in tiring himself physically. The mere fact of having put in words to another the conflict of the last few months seemed to have given actual existence to that which he had by fits and starts been trying to persuade himself was but a passing fancy. And even to himself he could not have told whether he was glad or sorry that the matter had come to a point—had, as it were, been taken out of his own hands. For that Madeline had already written to Mrs Englewood he felt little doubt.

"Women are always in such a desperate hurry," he said to himself, which, all things considered, was surely most unreasonable. Nor could he have denied that it was so, for even as he made the reflection he began to calculate in how many, or how few rather, days they might look for an answer, and to speculate on the chances of Mrs Englewood's being acquainted with Maisie's present whereabouts.

"Maisie," he called her to himself, though he had somehow shrunk from telling the name to his sister. It was so sweet—so likeher, he repeated softly, though, truth to tell, sweetness was not the most conspicuous quality in our heroine. But Despard was honestly in love after all, as many better and many worse men have been before him, and will be again. And love of the best kind, which on the whole his was, is clairvoyant—he was not wrong about Maisie's real sweetness.

"I do care for her, as deeply, as thoroughly as ever a man cared for a woman. But I don't want to marry; it's against all my plans and ideas. I didn't want to fall in love either, for that matter. The whole affair upsets everything I had ever dreamt of."

He felt dreaming now—he had managed to leave his sister and her friends, absorbed in the excitement of watching a game of lawn tennis between the best players of the county, and had stolen by himself down some shady walks away from the sparkle and chatter of the garden-party. The quiet and dimness soothed him, but increased the strange unreal feeling, of which he had been conscious since the morning. He felt as if nothing that could happen would surprise him—he was actually, in point of fact,not surprised, when at a turn in the path he saw suddenly before him, advancing towards him, her cloudy black drapery—for she was in black as ever—scarcely distinguishable from the dark shrubs at each side, the very person around whom all his thoughts were centring—Maisie—Maisie Ford herself!

He did not start, he made no exclamation. A strange intent look came into his eyes, as he walked on towards her. Long afterwards he remembered, and it helped to explain things, that she too had testified no surprise. But her face flushed a little, and the first expression he caught sight of was one of pleasure—afterwards, long afterwards, he remembered this too.

They met—their hands touched. But for a moment he did not speak.

"How do you do, Mr Norreys?" she said then. "It is hot and glaring on the lawn, is it not? I have just been seeing my father off. He was too tired to stay longer, and I was glad to wander about here in the shade a little."

"Your father?" he repeated half mechanically.

"Yes—we are staying, he and I, for a few days at Laxter's Hill. I am so sorry he has gone—I would so have liked you to see him."

She spoke eagerly, and with the peculiar, bright girlishness really natural to her, which was one of her greatest charms.

Despard looked at her; her voice and manner helped him a little to throw off the curious sensation of unreality. But he was, though he scarcely knew it, becoming inwardly more and more wrought up.

"I should have liked to see him exceedingly," he began, "any one so dear to you. I may hope some other time, perhaps, to do so? I—I was thinking of you when I first caught sight of you just now, Miss Ford—indeed, I have done nothing—upon my word, you may believe me—I have done little else than think of you since we last met."

The girl's face grew strangely still and intent, yet with a wistful look in the eyes telling of feelings not to be easily read. It was as if she were listening, in spite of herself, for something she still vaguely hoped she was mistaken in expecting.

"Indeed," she began to say, but he interrupted her.

"No," he said, "do not speak till you have heard me. I had made up my mind to it before I met you just now. I was just wondering how and when it could be. But now that this opportunity has come so quickly I will not lose it. I love you—I have loved you for longer than I knew myself, than I would own to myself—"

"From the very first, from that evening at Mrs Englewood's?" she said, and but for his intense preoccupation, he would have been startled by her tone.

"Yes," he said simply, yet with a strain of retrospection in his eyes, as if determined to control himself and speak nothing but the unexaggerated truth—"yes, I almost think it began that first evening, rude, brutally rude as I was to you. I would not own it—I struggled against it, for I did not want to marry. I had no thought of it. I am selfish, very selfish, I fear, and I preferred to keep clear of all ties and responsibilities, which too often become terribly galling on small means. I am no hero—but now—you will forgive my hesitation and—and reluctance, will you not? You are generous I know, and my frankness will not injure me with you, will it? You will believe that I loved you almost from the first, though I could not all at once make up my mind to marrying on small means? And now—now that I understand—that—that all seems different to me—that nothing seems of consequence except to hear you say you love me, as—as I have thought sometimes—Maisie—you will not be hard on me?—"

He stopped; he could have gone on much longer, and there was nothing now outwardly to interrupt him. She had stood there motionless, listening. Her face he could scarcely see, it was half turned away, but that seemed not unnatural. What then caused his sudden misgiving?

"Maisie," he repeated more timidly.

Then she turned—there was a burning spot of red on each cheek, her eyes were flaming. Yet her voice was low and quiet.

"Hard on you!" she repeated. "I am too sorry for myself to think or care much about you. I am—yes, I may own it, I am so horribly disappointed. I had really allowed myself to think of you as sincere, as, in spite of your unmanly affections, your contemptible conceit, an honest man, a possible friend I was beginning to forgive your ill-bred insolence to me as a stranger at the first, thinking there was something worthy of respect about you after all. But — oh, dear! And to try to humbug me by this sham honesty — to dare to say you did not think you could have cared for me enough to risk curtailing your own self-indulgences, but that now — it is too pitiful. But, oh, dear — it is too horribly disappointing!"

And as she looked at him again, he saw that her eyes were actually full of tears.

His brain was in a whirl of bewilderment, bitterest mortification and indignation. For the moment the last had the best of it.

"You have a right to refuse me, to despise my weakness if you choose — whether it is generous to take advantage of my misplaced confidence in you in having told you all — yes, all, is another matter. But one thing you shall not accuse me of, and that is, of lying to you. I have not said one untruthful word. I did — yes, I did love you, Mary Ford — what I feel to you now is something more like — "

He hesitated.

"Hate, I suppose," she suggested mockingly. "All the better. It cannot be a pleasant feeling to hate any one, and I do not wish you anything pleasant. If I could believe," she went on slowly, "if I could believe you had loved me, I think I should be glad, for it would be what you deserve. I would have liked to make you love me from that very first evening if I could — just to but unluckily I am not the sort of woman to succeed in anything of that kind. However — "

She stopped; steps approaching them were heard through the stillness. Maisie turned. "I have nothing more to say, and I do not suppose you wish to continue this conversation. Good-bye, Mr Norreys."

And almost before he knew she had gone, she had quite disappeared.

Despard was a strong man, but for a moment or two he really thought he was going to faint. He had grown deathly white while Maisie's hard, bitter words rained down upon him like hailstones; now that she had left him he grew so giddy that, had he not suddenly caught hold of a tree, he would have fallen.

"It feels like a sunstroke," he said vaguely to himself, as he realised that his senses were deserting him, not knowing that he spoke aloud.

He did not know either that some one had seen him stagger, and almost fall. A slightly uneasy feeling had made Maisie stop as she hurried off and glance back, herself unobserved.

"He looked so fearfully white," she said; "do—do men always look like that when girls refuse them, I wonder?"

For Maisie's experience of such things actually coming to the point, was, as should be the case with all true women, but small.

"I thought—I used to think I would enjoy seeing him humbled. But he did seem in earnest."

And then came the glimpse of the young fellow's physical discomfiture. Maisie was horribly frightened; throwing all considerations but those of humanity to the winds she rushed back again.

"Perhaps he has heart-disease, though he looks so strong," she thought, "and if so—oh, perhaps I have killed him."

She was beside him in an instant. A rustic bench, which Despard was too dizzy to see, stood near. The girl seized hold of his arm and half drew it round her shoulder. He let her do so unresistingly.

"Try to walk a step or two, Mr Norreys," she said, "I am very strong. There, now," as he obeyed her mechanically, "here is a seat," and she somehow half pushed, half drew him on to it. "Please smell this," and she took out a little silver vinaigrette, of strong and pungent contents, "I am never without this, for papa is so delicate, you know."

Despard tried to open his eyes, tried to speak, but the attempt was not very successful. Maisie held the vinaigrette close to his nose; he started back, the strong essence revived him almost at once. He took it into his own hand and smelt it again. Then his face grew crimson.

"I beg your pardon a thousand times. I am most ashamed, utterly ashamed of myself," he began.

But Maisie was too practically interested in his recovery to feel embarrassed.

"Keep sniffing at that thing," she said, "you will soon be all right. Only just tell me—" she added anxiously, "there isn't anything wrong with your heart, is there?"

"For if so," she added to herself, "I must at all costs run and see if there is a doctor to be had."

Despard smiled—a successfully bitter smile.

"No, thank you," he said. "I am surprised that you credit me with possessing one," he could not resist adding. "The real cause of this absurd faintness is a very prosaic one, I fancy. I went a long walk in the hot sun this morning."

"Oh, indeed, that quite explains it," said Maisie, slightly nettled. "Good-bye again then," and for the second time she ran off.

"All the same, I will get Conrad or somebody to come round that way," she said to herself. "I will just say I saw a man looking as if he was fainting. He won't be likely to tell."

And Despard sat there looking at the little silver toy in his bands.

"I did not thank her," he said to himself. "I suppose I should have done so, though she would have done as much, or more, for a starving tramp on the road."

Then he heard again steps coming nearer like those which had startled Maisie away.

They had apparently turned off elsewhere the first time—this time they came steadily on.

## Chapter Four.

As Despard heard the steps coming nearer he looked round uneasily, with a vague idea of hurrying off so as to escape observation. But when he tried to stand up and walk, he found that anything like quick movement was beyond him still. So he sat down again, endeavouring to look as if nothing were the matter, and that he was merely resting.

Another moment or two, and a young man appeared, coming hastily along the path by which Despard had himself made his way into the shrubbery. He was quite young, two or three and twenty at most, fair, slight, and boyish-looking. He passed by Mr Norreys with but the slightest glance in his direction, but just as Despard was congratulating himself on this, the new-comer stopped short, hesitated, and then, turning round and lifting his hat, came up to him.

"Excuse me," he said, "do you know Lady Margaret—by sight? Has she passed this way?"

He spoke quickly, and Mr Norreys did not catch the surname.

"No," he replied, "I have not the honour of the lady's acquaintance."

"I beg your pardon," said the other. "I've been sent to look for her, and I can't find her anywhere." Then he turned, but again hesitated.

"There's nothing the matter, is there? You've not hurt yourself—or anything? You look rather—as if a cricket ball had hit you, you know."

Mr Norreys smiled.

"Thank you," he said. "I have got a frightful pain in my head. I was out too long in the sun this morning."

The boyish-looking man shook his head.

"Touch of sunstroke—eh? Stupid thing to do, standing in the sun this weather. Should take a parasol; I always do. Then I can't be of any service?"

"Yes," said Despard, as a sudden idea struck him. "If you happen to know my sister, Mrs Selby, by sight, I'd be eternally grateful to you if you would tell her I'm going home. I'll wait for her at the old church, would you say?"

"Don't know her, but I'll find her out. Mrs Selby, of Markerslea, I suppose? Well, take my advice, and keep on the shady side of the road."

"I shall go through the woods, thank you. My sister will understand."

With a friendly nod the young fellow went off.

Despard had been roused by the talk with him. He got up now and went slowly round to the back of the house—it was a place he had known in old days—thus avoiding all risk of coming across any of the guests. By a path behind the stables he made his way slowly into the woods, and in about half an hour's time he found himself where these ended at the high road, along which his sister must pass. There was a stile near, over which, through a field, lay a footpath to the church, known thereabouts as the old church, and here on the stile Mr Norreys seated himself to await Mrs Selby.

"I've managed that pretty neatly," he said, trying to imagine he was feeling as usual. "I wonder who that fellow was. He seemed to have heard Maddie's name though he did not know her."

He was perfectly clear in his head now, but the pain in it was racking. He tried not to think, but in vain. Clearer, and yet more clearly, stood out before his mind's eye the strange drama of that afternoon. And the more he thought of it, the more he looked at it, approaching it from every side, the more incapable he became of explaining Miss Ford's extraordinary conduct. The indignation which had at first blotted out almost all other feeling gradually gave way to his extreme perplexity.

"She had no sort of grounds for speaking to me as she did," he reflected. "Accusing me vaguely of unworthy motives—whatcould she mean?" Then a new idea struck him. "Some one has been making mischief," he thought: "that must be it, though what and how, I cannot conceive. Gertrude Englewood would not do it intentionally—but still—I saw that she was changed to me. I shall have it out with her. After all, I hope Madeline's letter has gone."

And a vague, very faint hope began to make itself felt that perhaps, after all, all was not lost. If she had been utterly misled about him—if—

He drew a deep breath, and looked round. It was the very sweetest moment of a summer's day existence, that at which late afternoon begins softly and silently to fade into early evening. There was an almost Sabbath stillness in the air, a tender suggestion of night's reluctant approach, and from where Despard sat the white headstones of some graves in the ancient churchyard were to be seen among the grass. The man felt strangely moved and humbled.

"If I could hope ever to win her," he thought, "I feel as if I had it in me to be a better man—I am not all selfish and worldly, Maisie—surely not? But what has made her judge me so cruelly? It is awful to remember what she said, and to imagine what sort of an opinion she must have of me to have been able to say it. For—no, that was not my contemptible conceit—" and his face flushed. "She was beginning to care for me. She is too generous to have remembered vindictively my insolence, for insolence it was, at the first. Besides, she said herself that she had been getting to like and trust me as a friend. Till to-day—has the change in her all come from what I said to-day? No girl can despise a man for the fact of his caring for her—what can it be? Good heavens, I feel as if I should go mad!"

And he wished that the pain in his head, which had somewhat subsided, would get worse again, if only it would stop his thinking.

But just then came the sound of wheels. In another moment Mrs Selby's pony-carriage was in sight. Despard got off his stile, and walked slowly down the road to meet her.

"So you faithless—" she began—for, to tell the truth, she had not attached much credence to the story which had reached her of the frightful headache—but she changed her tone the moment she caught sight of his face. "My poor boy, you do look ill!" she exclaimed. "I am so sorry. I would have come away at once if I had known."

"It doesn't matter," Despard replied, as he got into the carriage; "but did you not get my message?"

"Oh, yes; but I thought it was just that you were tired and bored. What in the matter, dear Despard? You don't look the least like yourself."

"I fancy it was the sun this morning," he said.

"But it's passing off, I think."

Madeline felt by no means sure that it was so.

"I am so sorry," she repeated, "and so vexed with myself. Do you know who the young man was that gave me your message?"

Despard shook his head.

"It was Mr Conrad Fforde, Lord Southwold's nephew and heir — heir at least to the title, but to little else."

"So I should suppose," said Norreys indifferently.

"The Southwolds are very poor."

"How queer that he knew your name if you have never met him before," said Mrs Selby. "But I dare say it's through the Flores-Carters; they're such great friends of mine, you know, and they are staying at Laxter's Hill as well as the Southwold party."

"Yes," Despard agreed, "he had evidently heard of you."

"And of you too in that case. People do so chatter in the country. The Carters are dying to get you there. They have got the Southwolds to promise to go to them next week. They — the Carter girls — are perfectly wild about Lady Margaret. I think it would be better taste not to make up to her so much; it does look as if it was because she was what she is, though I know it isn't really that. They get up these fits of enthusiasm. And she is very nice — not very pretty, you know, but wonderfully nice and unspoilt, considering."

"Unspoilt," repeated Despard. He was glad to keep his sister talking about indifferent matters. "I don't see that poor Lord Southwold's daughter has any reason to be spoilt."

"Oh, dear yes — didn't you know? I thought you knew everything of that kind. It appears that she is a tremendous heiress; I forget the figures. The fortune comes from her aunt's husband. Her mother's elder sister married an enormously wealthy man, and as they had no children or near relations on his side, he left all to this girl. Of course she and her father have always known it, but it has been kept very quiet. They have lived in the country six months of the year, and travelled the other six. She has been most carefully brought up and splendidly educated. But she has never been 'out' in society at all till this year."

"I never remember hearing of them in town," said Despard.

"Oh, Lord Southwold himself never goes out. He is dreadfully delicate—heart-disease, I think. But she—Lady Margaret—will be heard of now. It has all come out about her fortune now that he has come into the title. His cousin, the last earl, only died two months ago."

"And," said Despard, with a strange sensation, as if he were listening to some one else speaking rather than speaking himself, "till he came into the title, what was he called? He was the last man's cousin, you say?"

"Yes, of course; he was Mr Fforde—Fforde with two 'f's' and an 'e,' you know. It's the family name of the Southwolds. That young man—the one you spoke to—is Mr Conrad Fforde, as I told you. They say that—"

But a glance at her brother made her hesitate.

"Despard, is your head worse?" she asked anxiously.

"It comes on by fits and starts," he replied. "But don't mind; go on speaking. What were you going to say?"

"Oh, only about young Mr Fforde. They say he is to marry Lady Margaret; they are only second cousins. But I don't think he looks good enough for her. She seems such a womanly, nice-feeling girl. We had just been introduced when Mr Fforde came up with your message, and she wanted him to go back to you at once. But he said you would be gone already, and I—well, I didn't quite believe about your head being so bad, and perhaps I seemed very cool about it, for Lady Margaret really looked quite vexed. Wasn't it nice of her? The Carters had been telling her about us evidently. I think she was rather disappointed not to see the famous Despard Norreys, do you know? I rather wonder you never met her this summer in town, though perhaps you would scarcely have remarked her just as Miss Fforde, for she isn't—"

But an exclamation from Despard startled her.

"Maddie," he said, "don't you understand? It must be she—she, this Lady Margaret—the great heiress! Good heavens!"

Mrs Selby almost screamed.

"Despard!" was all she could say. But she quickly recovered herself. "Well, after all," she went on, "I don't see that there's any harm done. She will know that you were absolutely disinterested, and surely that will go a long way. But—just to think of it! Oh, Despard, fancy your saying that you half thought she was going to be a governess! Oh, dear, how extraordinary! And I that was so regretting that you had not met her! What a good thing you did not—I mean what a good thing that my letter showing your ignorance was written and sent before you knew who she was! Don't you see how lucky it was?"

She turned round, her eyes sparkling with excitement and eagerness. But there was no response in Mr Norreys' face; on the contrary, its expression was such that Mrs Selby's own face grew pale with dread.

"Despard," she said, "why do you look like that? You are not going to say that now, because she is an heiress—just because ofmoney," with a tone of supreme contempt, "that you will give it up? You surely—"

But Mr Norreys interrupted her.

"Has the letter gone, Maddie?"

She nodded her head.

"Then I must write again at once—myself—to Gertrude Englewood to make her promise on her honour never to tell what you wrote. Even if I thought she would believe it—and I am not sure that she would—I could never allow myself to be cleared in her eyes now."

Madeline stared at him. Had the sunstroke affected his brain?

"Despard," she said, "what do you mean?"

He turned his haggard face towards her.

"I don't know how to tell you," he said. "I wish I need not, but as you know so much I must. I did see her, Madeline. I met her when I was strolling about the shrubbery over there. She was quite alone and no one near. It seemed to have happened on purpose, and—I told her all."

"You proposed to her?"

He nodded.

"As—as Miss Fforde, or as—" began Mrs

Selby.

"As Miss Ford, of course, without the two 'f's' and the 'e' at the end," he said bitterly. "I didn't know till this moment either that her father was an earl, or, which is much worse, that she was a great heiress."

"And what is wrong, then?"

"Just that she refused me—refused me with the most biting contempt—the—the bitterest scorn—no, I cannot speak of it. She thought I knew, had found out about her—and now I see that my misplaced honesty, the way I spoke, must have given colour to it. She taunted me with my insolence at the first—good God! what an instrument of torture a woman's tongue can be! There is only one thing to do—to stop Gertrude's ever telling of that letter."

"Oh, Despard!" exclaimed Mrs Selby, and her eyes filled with tears. "What a horrid girl she must be! And I thought she looked so sweet and nice. She seemed so sorry when her cousin told me about you. Tell me, was that after? Oh, yes, of course, it must have been. Despard, I believe she was already repenting her cruelty."

"Hush, Madeline," said Mr Norreys sternly. "You mean it well, but—you must promise me never to allude to all this again. You will show me Mrs Englewood's letter when it comes—that you must do, and I will write to her. But there is no more to be said. Let to-day be between us as if it had never been. Promise me, dear."

He laid his hand on her arm. Madeline turned her tearful eyes towards him.

"Very well," she said. "I must, I suppose. But, oh, what a dreadful pity it all seems. You to have fallen in love with her for herself — you that have never really cared for any one before — when you thought her only a governess; and now for it to have all gone wrong! It would have been so nice and delightful."

"A sort of Lord Burleigh business, with the characters reversed — yes, quite idyllic," said Despard sneeringly.

"Despard, don't. It does so pain me," Mrs Selby said with real feeling. "There is one person I am furious with," she went on in a very different tone, "and that is Mrs Englewood. She had no business to play that sort of trick."

"Perhaps she could not help herself. You say the father — Mr Fforde as he then was — did not wish her to be known as an heiress," said Mr Norreys.

"She might have made an exception for you," said Madeline.

Despard's brows contracted. Mrs Selby thought it was from the pain in his head, but it was more than that. A vision rose before him of a sweet flushed girlish face, with gentle pleasure and appeal in the eyes — and of Gertrude's voice, "If you don't dance, will you talk to her? Anything to please her a little, you know."

"I think Gertrude did all she could. I believe she is a perfectly loyal and faithful friend," he said; "but for heaven's sake, Maddie, let us drop it for ever. I will write this evening to Gertrude myself, and that will be the last act in the drama."

No letter, however, was written to Mrs Englewood that evening — nor the next day, nor for that matter during the rest of the time that saw Despard Norreys a guest at Markerslea Rectory.

And several days passed after the morning that brought her reply to Mrs Selby's letter of inquiry, before the person it chiefly concerned was able to see it. For the pain in his head, the result of slight sunstroke in the first place, aggravated by unusual excitement, had culminated in a sharp attack which at one time was not many degrees removed from brain fever. The risk was tided over, however, and at no time was the young man in very serious danger. But Mrs Selby suffered quite as much as if he had been dying. She made up her mind that he would not recover, and as her special friends received direct information to that effect, it is not to be wondered at that the bad news flew fast.

It reached Laxter's Hill one morning in the week following Lady Denster's garden-party. It was the day which was to see the breaking-up of the party assembled there to meet Lord Southwold and his daughter, and it came in a letter to Edith Flores-Carter from Mrs Selby herself.

"Oh, dear," the girl ejaculated, her usually bright, not to say jolly-looking countenance clouding over as she spoke, "oh, dear, I'm so sorry for the Selbys — for Mrs Selby particularly. Just fancy, doesn't it seem awful — her brother's dying."

She glanced round the breakfast-table for sympathy: various expressions of it reached her.

"That fellow I found in the grounds at that place, is it?" inquired Mr Fforde. "I'm not surprised, he did look pretty bad, and he would walk home, and he hadn't even a parasol."

"Conrad, how can you be so unfeeling? I perfectly detest that horrid trick of joking about everything," said in sharp, indignant tones a young lady seated opposite him. It was Lady Margaret. Several people looked up in surprise.

"Beginning in good time," murmured a man near the end of the table.

"Why, do you believe in that? I don't," replied his companion in the same low tone.

Conrad looked across the table at his cousin in surprise.

"Come now, Maisie," he said, "you make me feel quite shy, scolding me so in company. And I'm sure I didn't mean to say anything witty at the poor chap's expense. If I did, it was quite by mistake I assure you."

"Anything 'witty' from you would be that, I can quite believe," Lady Margaret replied, smiling a little. But the smile was a feeble and forced one. Conrad saw, if no one else did, that his cousin was thoroughly put out, and he felt repentant, though he scarcely knew why.

Half an hour later Lord Southwold and his daughter were talking together in the sitting-room, where the former had been breakfasting in invalid fashion alone.

"I would promise to be home to-morrow, or the day after at latest, papa," Lady Margaret was saying; "Mrs Englewood will be very pleased to have me, I know, even at the shortest notice, for last week when I wrote saying I feared it would be impossible, she was very disappointed."

"Very well, my dear, only don't stay with her longer than that, for you know we have engagements," and Lord Southwold sighed a little.

Margaret sighed too.

"My darling," said her father, "don't look so depressed. I didn't mean to grumble."

"Oh no, papa. It isn't you at all. I shall be glad to be at home again; won't you? Thank you very much for letting me go round by town."

Mrs Englewood's drawing-room — but looking very different from the last time we saw it. Mrs Englewood herself, with a more anxious expression than usual on her pleasant face, was sitting by the open window, through which, however, but little air found its way, for it was hot, almost stifling weather.

"It is really a trial to have to come back to town before it is cooler," she was saying to herself, as the door opened and Lady Margaret, in summer travelling gear, came in.

"So you are really going, dear Maisie," said her hostess. "I do wish you could have waited another day."

"But," said Maisie, "you will let me know at once what you hear from Mrs Selby. I cannot help being unhappy, Gertrude, and, of course, what you have told me has made me still more self-reproachful, and — and ashamed."

She was very pale, but a sudden burning blush overspread her face as she said the last words.

"I do so hope he will recover," she added, trying to speak lightly, "though if he does I earnestly hope I shall never meet him again."

"Even if I succeed in making him understand your side, and showing him how generously you regret having misjudged him?" said Mrs Englewood. "I don't see that there need be any enmity between you."

"Not enmity, oh no; but still less, friendship," said Maisie. "I just trust we shall never meet again. Good-bye, dear Gertrude: I am so glad to have told you all. You will let me know what you hear?" and she kissed Mrs Englewood affectionately.

"Good-bye, dear child. I am glad you have not a long journey before you. Stretham will take good care of you. You quite understand that I can do nothing indirectly — it will only be when I see him himself that I can tell him how sorry you have been."

"Sorry and ashamed, be sure to say 'ashamed,'" said Lady Margaret: "yes, of course, it can only be if — if he gets better or you see him yourself."

Two or three days later came a letter to Lady Margaret from Mrs Englewood, inclosing one which that lady had just received from Mrs Selby. Her brother, she allowed for the first time, was out of danger, but "terribly weak." And at intervals during the next few weeks the girl heard news of Mr Norreys' recovery. And "I wonder," she began to say to herself, "I wonder if Gertrude has seen him, or will be seeing him soon."

But this hope, if hope it should be called, was doomed to disappointment. Late in October came another letter from her friend.

"I am sorry," wrote Mrs Englewood, "that I see no probability of my meeting Mr Norreys for a long time. He is going abroad. After all, your paths in life are not likely to cross each other again. Perhaps it is best to leave things."

But the tears filled Maisie's eyes as she read. "I should have liked him to know I had come to do him justice," she thought.

She did not understand Mrs Englewood's view of the matter.

"It would be cruel," Gertrude had said to herself, "to tell him how she blames herself, and how my showing her Mrs Selby's letter had cleared him. It would only bring it all up again when he has doubtless begun to forget it."

Nevertheless, Despard did not leave England without knowing how completely Lady Margaret had retracted her cruel words, and how bitterly she regretted them.

Time passes quickly, we are told, when we are hard at work. And doubtless this is true while the time in question is the present. But to look back upon time of which every day and every hour have been fully occupied, gives somewhat the feeling of a closely-printed volume when one has finished reading it. It seems even longer than in anticipation. To Despard Norreys, when at the end of two busy years he found himself again in England, it appeared as if he had been absent five or six times as long as was really the case.

He had been a week in England, and was still detained in town by details connected with the work he had successfully accomplished. He was under promise to his sister to run down to Markerslea the first day it should be possible, and time meanwhile hung somewhat heavily on his hands. The waters had already closed over his former place in society, and he did not regret it. Still there were friends whom he was glad to meet again, and so he not unwillingly accepted some of the invitations that began to find him out.

One evening, after dining at the house of the friend whose influence had obtained for him the appointment which had just expired, he accompanied the ladies of the family to an evening party in the neighbourhood. He had never been in the house before; the faces about him were unfamiliar. Feeling a little "out of it," he strolled into a small room where a select quartette was absorbed at whist, and seated himself in a corner somewhat out of the glare of light, which, since his illness, rather painfully affected his eyes.

Suddenly the thought of Maisie Fforde as he had last seen her seemed to rise before him as in a vision.

"I wonder if she is married," he said to himself. "Sure to be so, I should think. Yet I should probably have heard of it."

And even as the words formed themselves in his mind, a still familiar voice caught his ear.

"Thank you. Yes, this will do nicely. I will wait here till Mabel is ready to go."

And a lady — a girl, he soon saw — came forward into the room towards the corner where he was sitting. He rose at once; she approached him quickly, then with a sudden, incoherent exclamation, made as if she would have drawn back. But it was too late; she could not, if she wished, have pretended she did not see him.

"Mr Norreys," she began; "I had no idea —"

"That I was in England," he said. "No, I have only just returned. Pardon me for having startled you, Miss Fforde — Lady Margaret, I mean. I on my side had no idea of meeting you here or —"

"Or you would not have come," she in her turn interrupted him with. "Thank you; you are frank at all events," she added haughtily.

He turned away. There was perhaps some involuntary suggestion of reproach in his manner, for hers changed.

"No," she said. "I am very wrong. Please stay for two minutes, and listen to me. I have hoped and prayed that I might never meet you again, but at the same time I made a vow — a real vow," she went on girlishly, "that if I did so I would swallow my pride, and — and ask you to forgive me. There now — I have said it. That is all. Will you, Mr Norreys?"

He glanced round; the whist party was all unconscious of the rest of the world still —

"Will you not sit down for a moment, Lady Margaret?" he said, and as she did so he too drew a chair nearer to hers. "It is disagreeable to be overheard," he went on in a tone of half apology. "You ask me what I cannot now do," he added.

The girl reared her head, and the softness of her manner hardened at once.

"Then," she said, "we are quits. It does just as well. My conscience is clear now."

"So is mine, as to that particular of—of what you call forgiving you," he said, and his voice was a degree less calm. "I cannot do so now, for—I forgave you long, long ago."

"You have seen Mrs Englewood? She has told you at last that all was explained to me—your sister's letter and all," she went on confusedly, "that I saw how horrid, how low and mean and suspicious and everything I had been?"

"I knew all you refer to before I left England," he said simply. "But I asked Mrs Englewood to leave it as it was, unless she was absolutely forced to tell you. I knew you must hate the sound of my name, and she promised to drop the subject."

"And I have scarcely seen her for a long time," said Maisie. "I saw she did avoid it, and I suppose she thought it no use talking about it."

"I did not need her explanation," Despard went on gently. "I had—if you will have the word—I had forgiven you long before. Indeed, I think I did so almost at once. It was all natural on your part. What had I done, what was I that you should have thought any good of me? When you remembered the way I behaved to you at first," and here his voice grew very low. "I have never been able to—I shall never be able to forgive myself—"

"Mr Norreys!" said Maisie in a very contrite tone. But Despard kept silence.

"Are you going to stay at home now, or are you going away again?" she asked presently, trying to speak in a matter-of-fact way.

"I hardly know. I am waiting to see what I can get to do. I don't much mind what, but I shall never again be able to be idle," he said, smiling a little for the first time. "It is my own fault entirely—the fault of my own past folly—that I am not now well on in the profession I was intended for. So I must not grumble if I have to take what work I can get in any part of the world. I would rather stay in England for some reasons."

"Why?" she asked.

"I cannot stand heat very well," he said. "My little sunstroke left some weak points—my eyes are not strong."

She did not answer at once.

Then, "How crooked things are," she said at last suddenly; "you want work, and I—oh, I am so busy and worried. Papa impressed upon me that I must look after things myself, and accept the responsibilities, but—I don't think he quite saw how difficult it would be," and her eyes filled with tears.

"But—" said Despard, puzzled by her manner, "he is surely able to help you?"

She turned to him more fully—the tears came more quickly, but she did not mind his seeing them.

"Didn't you know?" she said; "Papa is dead—more than a year ago now. Just before I came of age. I am quite alone. That silly—I shouldn't say that, he is kind and good—Conrad is Lord Southwold now. But I don't want to marry him, though he is almost the only man who, I know, cares for me for myself. How strange you did not know about my being all alone! Didn't you notice this?" and she touched her black skirt.

"I have never seen you except in black," said Despard. "No—I had no idea. I am so grieved."

"If—if you stay in England," she began again half timidly, "and you say you have forgiven me,"—he made a little gesture of deprecation of the word—"can't we be friends, Mr Norreys?"

Despard rose to his feet. The whist party had dispersed. The little room was empty.

"No," he said, "I am afraid that could never be, Lady Margaret. The one reason why I wish to leave England again is that I know now, I cannot—I must not risk seeing you."

Maisie looked up, the tears were still glimmering about her eyes and cheeks; was it their soft glistening that made her face look so bright and almost radiant?

"Oh, do say it again—don't think me not nice, oh, don't!" she entreated. "But why—oh, why, if you care for me, though I can scarcely believe it, why let my horrible money come between us? I shall never care for anybody else—there now, I have said it!" And she tried to hide her face, but he would not let her.

"Do you really mean it, dear?" he said. "If you do, I—I will swallow my pride, too; shall I?"

She looked up, half laughing now.

"Quits again, you see. Oh, dear, how dreadfully happy I am! And you know, as you are so fond of work now, you will have lotsto do. All manner of things for poor people that I want to manage, and don't know how—and all our own—I won't say 'my' any more—tenants to look after—and—and—"

"'That girl in black' herself to take care of, and make as happy as all my love and my strength, and my life's devotion can," said Despard. "Maisie, my darling; God grant that you may never regret your generosity and goodness."

"No, no," she murmured, "yours are far greater, far, far greater."

There was a moment's silence. Then suddenly Despard put his hand into his pocket and held out something to Maisie.

"Look," he said, "do you remember? I should have returned it to you, but I could not make up my mind to it. I have never parted with it night or day, all these years."

It was the little silver vinaigrette.

This all happened several years ago, and, by what I can gather, there are few happier people than Despard Norreys and Lady Margaret, his wife.

# Chapter Five.

Bronzie.

It was in church I saw her first. She was seated some little way in front of me, somewhat to one side. My eyes had been roving about, I suppose, for I was only a boy, fifteen or thereabouts at most, and she was — let me see — she could not have been more than nine, though by the pose of her head, the dignity of the small figure altogether, the immaculate demeanour — which said all over her, "I am in church, and behaving myself accordingly" — one might well have taken her for at least five years older.

I remember positively starting when I first caught sight of her — of it, I should rather say; for her, in the ordinary sense of seeing a person — that is to say, her face — I never once saw during the whole of the first stage of our one-sided acquaintance — the first act of the drama, so to speak. The "it" was her hair. Never — never before or since, I do verily believe, has such hair gladdened mortal eyes. "Golden" was no word for it, or, rather, was but one of the many words it suggested. It was in great floods of waving and wavering shades of reddish — reddish, not red, mind you — brown, dark brown. The mass of it was certainly dark, though the little golden lights gleamed out all over as you will see the sparkling threads of the precious metal ever and anon through the texture of some rich antique silk with which they are cunningly interwoven. I worried myself to find an adjective in any sense suitable for this marvellous colour, or colours; but it was no use, and at last, in a sort of despair, I hit upon the very inadequate but not unsuggestive one of "bronze." It seemed to come a degree nearer it than any other, and it struck me, too, as not commonplace. From "bronze" I went a step further; I found I must have a name for her — a same all my own, that no one would understand even if they heard it; and, half without knowing it, I slipped into calling her to myself, into thinking of my little lady-love as "Bronzie." For I had fallen in love with her — looking back now I am sure of it — I had fallen in love with her in the sweet, vague, wholly ridiculous, wholly poetical way that a boy falls in love. And yet I had never seen her face; nay, stranger still, I did not want to see it!

It was not so at first; for two or three Sundays after the fateful one on which the glorious hair dazzled me into fairy-land, my one idea was to catch sight of Bronzie's face. But from where I sat it was all but impossible; she wore a shady hat, too—a hat with a long ostrich feather drooping over the left side, which much increased the difficulty. In time, and with patience, no doubt I should have succeeded; but, as I have said, before long the wish to succeed left me. I was only in London for my Christmas holidays, and, somehow, I fancied that Bronzie, too, was but a visitor there.

"I shall never see her again," I reflected, with a certain sentimental enjoyment of the thought; "but I can always think of her. And if her face were not in accordance with her hair and her figure—that dear little dignified, erect figure—what a disappointment! If she had an ugly mouth, or if she squinted, or even if she were just commonplace and expressionless—no, I don't want to see her."

Accident favoured me; all those Sundays, as I have said, I never did see her face. The church was crowded; we made our exit by different aisles, and, as I was staying with cousins who were never in time for anything, we always came in late—later than Bronzie, any way. The little figure, the radiant hair, were always there in the same corner for my eyes to rest upon from the moment I ensconced myself in my place. And so it was to the end of the holidays—somewhat longer that year than usual, from illness of an infectious nature, having broken out among the brothers and sisters at my home.

I went back to school, to Latin verses and football, to the mingled work and play which make up the intense present of a boy's life; I was, to all appearance, just the same as before, and yet I was changed. I never talked about my Bronzie to any one, I made up no dreams about her, built no castles in the air of ever seeing her again, and yet I never forgot her. No, truly, strange and almost incredible as it may seem, I never did forget her; I feel almost certain there was no day in which the remembrance of her did not flash across my mental vision.

It was three years later. School-days were over—so recently over that I had scarcely realised the fact, not, certainly, to the extent of feeling sad or pathetic about it—such regrets come afterwards, and come to stay; my feeling was rather one of rejoicing in my new liberty, and pride in being considered man enough to escort an elder sister on a somewhat distant journey had effectually put everything else out of my head that Christmas-time—it was always at Christmas-time—when—I saw heragain. We were at a railway station, a junction; our through carriage was being shunted and bumped about in the mysterious way peculiar to those privileged vehicles. We had been "sided" into a part of the station different from that where we had arrived; I was leaning out, staring about me, when suddenly, some little way off, there gleamed upon me for a moment the glow of that wonderful hair. The platform was crowded; Bronzie was walking away in an opposite direction, though slowly. She was with two ladies; as usual, it was only the hair and figure I saw—no glimpse of the face was possible; yet I knew it was she. Nor, of course, would the sight of a face I never had seen have helped to identify her.

"By Jove!" I exclaimed aloud, unconscious that my sister was close behind me; "by Jove! how she has grown!"

"Who?" Isabel exclaimed; "whom are you speaking of? Is there some one there we know?" and in another instant she too was craning her neck out of the window. "I don't see any one," she added, withdrawing her head, in disappointment. "Who was it, Vic?"

I think I had turned pale; I felt myself now grow crimson.

"Oh!" I blurted out, saying, of course, in my confusion exactly what I would not have said: "only a—a little girl with such wonderful hair."

"Where?" asked Isabel, again poking her head out—in the wrong direction, of course; she was tired of the long waiting, and jumped at the smallest excitement. "Oh, yes! I see! at the door of the refreshment, room. Yes, it is magnificent hair; but, Vic, you said—"

"Nonsense!" I interrupted, "she's nowhere near the refreshment room; it's not possible it's the same."

Nor was it. Bronzie was by this time out of sight, far off among the throng of travellers at the left extremity of the platform, and the refreshment room was some yards to our right. It was absolutely, practically impossible. "Nonsense!" I repeated peevishly, looking out, nevertheless, in expectation of seeing some childish head of ordinary fair hair at the spot my sister indicated. But I started violently—yes, it was Bronzie again; the self-same hair, at least. And the girl was standing, with her back to us, at the door of the first-class refreshment room, as Isabel had said. I felt as if I were dreaming; my brain was in a whirl. I sat down in my place for a moment to recover myself.

"I wonder," said my sister, "if her face is as lovely as her hair? She is sure to turn round directly. Wait a minute, Vic, I'll tell you if she oh, how tiresome! I do believe we are off; after waiting so long, they might as well have waited one moment longer."

And off we were—in the opposite direction too. We could see no more of her—Bronzie, or not Bronzie! On the whole I was not sorry that my sister's curiosity was doomed to be unsatisfied. But my own perplexity was great. How could the child have been spirited all the length of the station in that instant of time?

"She is a fairy; that is the only explanation," I said to myself, laughingly. "Perhaps I have dreamt her only—in church, that Christmas too—but no; Isabel saw the hair as well as I."

Time went on, faster and faster. I was a man—very thoroughly a man—for seven years had passed since that winter day's journey. I was five-and-twenty; I had completed my studies, travelled for a couple of years, and was about settling down to my own home and its responsibilities—for my father was dead, and I was an eldest son—when the curtain rises for the third and last time in this simplest of dramas. I was unmarried, yet no misogamist, nor was there the shadowiest of reasons why I should not marry; rather, considerably even, the other way. My family wished it; I wished it myself in the abstract. I had money enough and to spare. I loved my home, and was ready to love it still more; but I had never cared for any woman as I knew I must care for the woman I could make happy, and be happy with, as my wife. It was strange—strange and disappointing. I had never fallen in love, though I may really say I had wished to do so. Never,

that is to say since I was fifteen, and the gleaming locks of my Bronzie —
like Aslauga's golden tresses — had irradiated for me the corner of the
gloomy old London church where she sat.

That was ten years ago now, yet I had not forgotten my one bit of romance.

It was Christmas again. For the day itself I was due at home, of course; but
on the way thither I had promised to spend a night with Greatrex, a friend
of some few years' standing, whom I had not seen since his marriage, at
which something or other had prevented my being present. He had invited
me before, but I had not felt specially keen about it. He was rapturously in
love with his wife I could see by his letters, and that sort of thing, under the
circumstances, made me feel rather "out in the cold" — not unnaturally. But
at last I had given in: I was to stay a night, possibly two, at Moresham,
Greatrex's home, where, as he had written, on receiving my acceptance,
"You will see her at last," for all the world as if I had been dying to behold
Mrs Greatrex, and counting the hours till my longings for this privilege
should be gratified.

Greatrex met me at the door. It was afternoon, but clear daylight still,
though December, when I drove up.

"So delighted, so uncommonly pleased, old fellow, at last," he ejaculated,
shaking me vigorously by the hand; "and so will Bessie be. I don't know
much about your taste, but you can't but agree that I have shown some,
when you see her. One of her great beauties is her hair; I wonder if you'll
like the way she—; what's the matter?" as the footman interrupted him
with a "Beg pardon, sir," "Oh yes, I'll tell Barnes myself;" and he turned
back to the groom, still at the door. "Excuse me one instant, old fellow.
Bessie is in the drawing-room."

"Don't announce me. I will introduce myself," I said hastily to the servant.
A queer, a very queer feeling had come over me, at that mention, by her
husband, of Mrs Greatrex's hair — could it be? And her name was Bessie. I
could not imagine Bronzie by that name — my stately little maiden — what if
it were though? and my dream to end thus?

I stepped quietly into the room. She was standing by the window; there was snow outside. I saw her, all but her face, perfectly: I saw it — the hair — and for an instant I felt positively faint. It was it — it must be she; the way she wore it was peculiar, though very graceful; the head was pretty, but the small figure, though neat and well proportioned, was by no means what I had pictured Bronzie as a woman. But what did it matter? She was Greatrex's wife.

"I must introduce myself; Mrs Greatrex," I began, and then, as my words caught her ears, she turned, and for the first time I saw the face — the face I had so often pictured as a fit accompaniment to that glorious hair.

Oh, the disappointment — the strange disappointment — and yet the still stranger relief! For she was Greatrex's wife! But she wasn't Bronzie — my Bronzie had never been. There was no Bronzie!

Yet it was a sweet and a pretty little face, and a good little face too. Now that I know it well I do not hesitate to call it a very dear and charming little face, though the features are only pretty; the eyes nothing particular, except for their pleasant expression; the nose distinctly insignificant.

I exerted myself to be agreeable. When Greatrex came in, a moment or two afterwards, he was evidently quite satisfied as to the terms on which we already stood. Then followed afternoon tea. It seemed to go to my head. I felt curiously excited, reckless, and almost bitter, and yet unable mentally to drop the subject as it were. The absurdity of the whole filled me with a sort of contempt for myself, and still there was a fascination about it. I determined to go through with it, to punish myself well for my own fantastic nonsense, to show my own folly up to myself.

"You may be surprised, Mrs Greatrex," I said, suddenly, "to hear that — I feel sure I am not mistaken in saying so — that I have seen you before."

She was surprised, but she smiled pleasantly.

"Indeed," she said; while "where? when? Let's hear all about it. Why didn't you tell us before?" exclaimed Greatrex, in his rather clumsy way.

"Can you carry your memory back, let me see, nine, ten years?" I asked. "Do you remember if at that time you spent a winter in London; or was London your home?"

She shook her head. "No, it was not; but I did spend the winter of in London."

"Had you — can you possibly recollect if you wore a large, rather slouching, felt hat, with a long feather — grey, the hat, too, was grey — that fell over the left side? and a coat of grey, too, some kind of velvet, I think, trimmed with dark fur?"

Greatrex looked extremely astonished.

"Come, now," he ejaculated.

Mrs Bessie smiled.

"Yes," she said, "I remember the whole get-up perfectly."

Greatrex looked triumphant. I did not, for I did not feel so.

"And," I went on listlessly, almost — I felt so sure of it now — "did you not come to church for several Sundays that winter; and on Christmas Day, to Saint Edric's, in — Square?"

For the first time Mrs Greatrex shook her head.

"No," she said. "I never remember being in Saint Edric's in my life."

Greatrex's face fell; he had been quite excited and delighted, poor fellow.

"Come, now," he said again, in a different tone, "are you sure, Bessie? I think you must be mistaken."

"I think so, too," I added, a little more eager myself now. "You may have forgotten the name. Saint Edric's is — " and I went on to describe the church.

"You came with a lady who looked like a governess," and I concluded with some details as to this person's appearance.

"Yes," Mrs Greatrex said, "that sounds like our governess — Mrs Mills; she was with us several years. But it is not only that I was never at Saint

Edric's; I was never at church all those weeks in London at all. I had a bad attack of bronchitis. I remember particularly how vexed I was not to wear my new things, especially as we—" suddenly a curious change of expression came over her face, and just at that instant her husband interrupted her.

"I have it," he began excitedly, but he got no farther. "Bessie," he exclaimed, with almost a shriek, "my dearest child, you've scalded me!" and he looked up ruefully from the contents of a cup of tea deposited on his knee.

"No, no," his wife exclaimed, "it was only a little water I was pouring into my cup, and it was not very hot. But come along, I have a cloth in the conservatory, where I was arranging some flowers. I'll rub it dry in an instant."

She almost dragged him off—with unnecessary vehemence, it seemed to me. I could not make her out. "An odd little woman," I thought. "I hope, for Greatrex's sake, she's not given to nerves or hysterics, or that sort of thing."

But they were back in two minutes, Greatrex quite smiling and content, though he has owned to me since that his knee wasscalded, all the same.

No more was said on the subject of reminiscences. Indeed, it seemed to me that Bessie rather avoided it, and a new idea struck me—perhaps Greatrex was given to frightful jealousy, though he hid it so well, and his wife had got him off into the conservatory to smooth him down. Yes, his manner was queer. Poor little woman! I forgave her her hair.

We strolled off to the stables, then to have a smoke, and thus idled away the time till the dressing-bell rang.

"We're very punctual people," said Greatrex, as he showed me to my room.

So I made haste, and found myself entering the drawing-room some few minutes before the hands of my watch had reached the dinner-hour.

"She is punctual," I thought, as I caught sight of a white-robed figure standing with its back to me, full in the light of a suspended lamp, whose rays caught the gleam of her radiant hair. "Not—not very wise to be down before him, if he has the uncomfortable peculiarity that I suspect. By Jove! how much taller she looks in evening dress! Strange that it should make such a difference!"

"So your husband is the laggard, in spite of his boasted punctuality, Mrs Greatrex?" I began.

She turned towards me.

"I am not Mrs Greatrex," she said, while she raised her soft brown eyes to my face, and a little colour stole into her cheeks.

The words were unnecessary. I stood silent, motionless, spell-bound.

"I—I am only her sister—Imogen Grey," she went on.

I have asked her since if she thought me mad: she says not; but I feel as if I must have seemed so. For still I could not speak, though certain words seemed dancing like happy fairies across my brain. "Bronzie, my Bronzie! found at last. Bronzie!"

And in another instant good little Bessie Greatrex was in the room, busy introducing me to her sister, "Miss Grey," and explaining that she had not been sure of Imogen's arriving in time for dinner—had I heard the wheels just as we went up to dress?

She was a little confused; but it was not till afterwards that I thought of it. In a sort of dream I went in to dinner; in a sort of dream I went through that wonderful evening. They were as unlike as sisters could well be, except for the hair: unlike, and yet alike; for, if there is one woman in this world as good and true as my Bronzie, it is her sister Bessie.

Yes, she was—she is my Bronzie, though no one knows the name, nor the whole story, but our two happy selves.

And I had it out with Bessie; she suspected the truth while I was questioning her about her recollections, and then she saw it must have been Imogen, and not herself: the dragging off poor Greatrex into the conservatory was to tell him to hold his tongue. She wanted so to "surprise" me! I believe, at the bottom of my heart, that Greatrex and she had planned something of the kind even before they heard my unexpected reminiscences; and if they did, there was no harm in it. But—if she hadn't been my Bronzie, nothing would have been any use; I should have lived and died unmarried.